WRIGGLY PIG

2

2

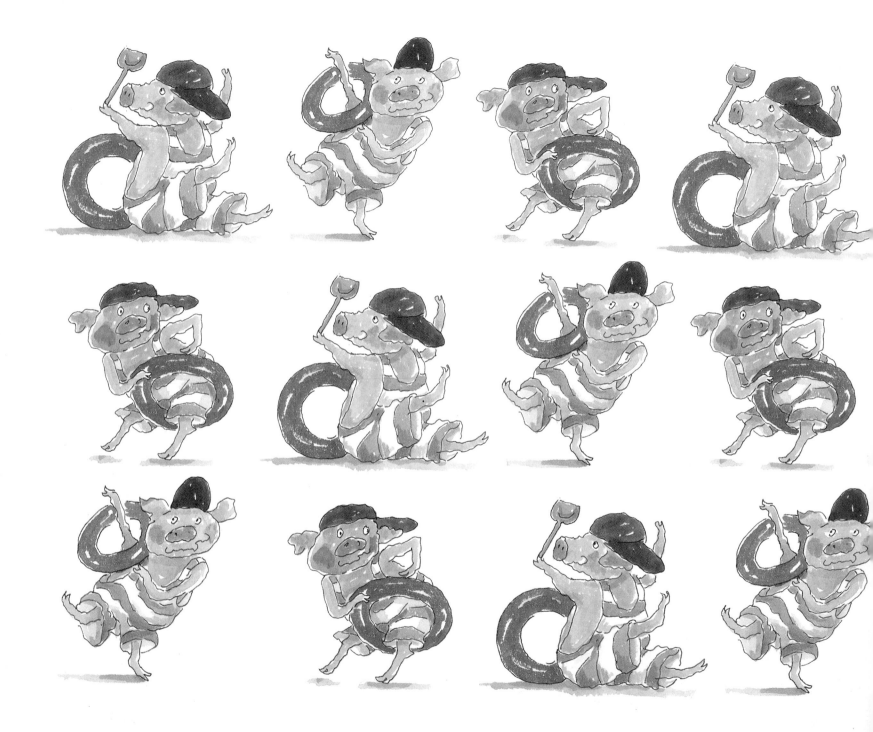

For Matthew, with love   S.J.P.

A Red Fox Book

Published by Random House Children's Books
20 Vauxhall Bridge Road, London SW1V 2SA

A division of Random House UK Ltd.
London Melbourne Sydney Auckland
Johannesburg and agencies throughout the world

First published by Hutchinson Children's Books 1991

Red Fox edition 1993

Text copyright © Jon Blake 1991
Illustrations © Susie Jenkin-Pearce 1991

Printed in Hong Kong

ISBN 0 09 973770 1

WRIGGLY PIG

Story by Jon Blake
Illustrated by Susie Jenkin-Pearce

RED FOX

The Pigs were getting ready for their afternoon out. Mr Trevor Pig was ready.

Mrs Hetty Pig was ready.

Daniel Pig was ready, and Charlotte Pig was ready. But Wriggly Pig was not ready.

'Keep still, Wriggly Pig!' said Trevor Pig, as he buttoned Wriggly's jacket.

But Wriggly Pig would not keep still.

'He should have been a worm,' said Hetty Pig.

The Pigs set off in the car. Daniel Pig sat straight and looked out of the left window. Charlotte Pig sat even straighter and looked out of the right window. But Wriggly Pig fidgeted and squirmed, and tried to look out of all the windows at once.

'Keep still, Wriggly Pig!' said Hetty Pig. 'I can't see the cars behind!'
But Wriggly Pig would not keep still.

   'He's got ants in his pants,' said Trevor Pig.

The Pigs arrived at the cinema.
Soon Hetty and Trevor and
Charlotte and Daniel were glued
to the screen.

But Wriggly Pig was not glued
to anything. He shuffled, and
shifted, and rustled his popcorn.

'Keep still, Wriggly Pig!' said
the goats behind. 'We can't see
the picture!'

But Wriggly Pig would not
keep still. Soon everybody in the
cinema was moaning and
groaning: 'Keep still, Wriggly Pig!'

The Pigs had no choice but to
get up and go.

The Pigs decided to go to the beach instead. Soon Trevor and Hetty were drifting off to sleep in the warm, peaceful sun.

But Wriggly Pig could not see the point of sleeping in the middle of the day. He tossed and turned, and sent showers of sand all over the place.

'Keep still, Wriggly Pig!' said
Daniel Pig. 'You're getting sand in
the lunch box.'

But Wriggly Pig would not
keep still. There was sand in the
sandwiches, sand in the

lemonade, and sand in Trevor
Pig's ear.

'That's it!' said Trevor Pig.
'We'll go somewhere where
there's no sand.'

The Pigs arrived at the putting green. They lined up with their putters at the first hole. It was Charlotte's go first. Hetty Pig said 'Ssh!'. Trevor and Daniel were quiet as mice. But Wriggly Pig was not quiet. Wriggly Pig hummed and whistled, and swung with his putter.

'Keep still, Wriggly Pig!' said Charlotte Pig. 'You'll put me off!'

But Wriggly Pig would not keep still. He made Charlotte so nervy, she hit her ball right over the wall. There was a loud SMASH!

'That's your fault, Wriggly Pig!' said Charlotte; and the Pigs ran as fast as they could, back to the car.

The Pigs were getting very fed up. They decided to go to a café.

It was a polite kind of café, where everyone spoke softly and sat neatly. Everyone, that is, except for Wriggly Pig. He played with the menu and tugged at the tablecloth, and scratched at his shoulderblade.

"Keep still, Wriggly Pig!' said Hetty Pig. 'Everyone will think we've got fleas!'

The sheep at the next table heard Hetty say 'fleas'. They looked at Wriggly Pig, they looked at each other, then they got up and left.

Soon there was no-one in the café but the Pigs. 'That's the last straw, Wriggly Pig!' said Hetty Pig. 'We're taking you to see a doctor!'

Wriggly Pig did not like the doctor's surgery. He quivered and trembled and wriggled more than usual.

'Hmm,' said the doctor. 'It sounds like Wriggle Fever. Or it may be Fidget-itis. I shall have to examine this pig.'

Wriggly Pig did not want to be
examined.

'Keep still, Wriggly Pig!' said
the doctor, and he pressed his
cold, cold hoofs on Wriggly's
belly.

That was enough for Wriggly
Pig. He leapt off the table, dived
through the doctor's legs, and
vanished through the door.

Wriggly Pig had never run so fast in his life. He raced down the stairs,

through the waiting room,

and out onto the street.

He sped down the pavement with his trotters flying,

hurtled round the corner ... and went BANG! straight into a postbox.

Wriggly Pig lay very still.

'Are you all right, Wriggly Pig?' asked Hetty Pig. Wriggly Pig did not answer.

'Wake up, Wriggly Pig!' said Trevor Pig.

Wriggly did not move a muscle.

Trevor, and Hetty, and Charlotte, and Daniel began to feel very upset.

Then Wriggly's ear twitched.

His snout gave a sniff.

His tail gave a wiggle,

and his eye opened.

Soon Wriggly Pig was wriggling
all over. He wriggled more than
the wriggliest worm and the
squirmiest snake.

The Pigs breathed a sigh of
relief. They hugged Wriggly,
then they hugged
each other.

'From now on,' said Wriggly Pig, 'I really will try to keep still.'
'No!' said the other Pigs. 'Keep wriggling, Wriggly Pig!' And the whole family wriggled all the way home.